Bunny Trouble Treasury

To
Luke
♥ Hans Wilhelm

Bunny Trouble Treasury

Hans Wilhelm

Dover Publications, Inc.
Mineola, New York

Bibliographical Note

Bunny Trouble Treasury, first published by Dover Publications, Inc., in 2014, is
a new compilation of the following works: *Bunny Trouble, More Bunny Trouble,*
and *Bad, Bad Bunny Trouble,* written and illustrated by Hans Wilhelm, originally
published by Scholastic, Inc., New York, in 1985, 1989, and 1994; and *Ten Little
Bunnies,* written by Nurit Karlin and illustrated by Hans Wilhelm, originally
published by Simon & Schuster, New York, in 1994.

International Standard Book Number

ISBN-13: 978-0-486-49275-9
ISBN-10: 0-486-49275-3

Manufactured in the United States by Courier Corporation
49275301   2014
www.doverpublications.com

CONTENTS

BUNNY
TROUBLE

Once there was a rabbit colony that was different from any other. The rabbits here were in charge of decorating all the Easter eggs for the Easter Bunny to deliver.

Everyone worked year-round getting ready.

3

Everyone except Ralph. He cared for only one
thing in the world—soccer.

It worried his father and mother.

It worried the other rabbits in the colony.

It worried his teachers in the school where all the young rabbits went to learn egg decorating. Where was Ralph while everyone else was hard at work in the classroom? He was outside working on his fancy footwork.

It worried his sister Liza—especially when he ruined her birthday party.

Liza loved Ralph more than anyone else in the world. But she knew that one day he would get in trouble. He just didn't fit in.

Each year as Easter approached, everyone got busier and busier. The chickens laid more eggs. The painters, the jelly bean makers, and the basket stuffers all worked overtime.

12

Ralph had to work, too. But he had a hard time keeping his mind on his job.

Instead, he was thinking about place kicks, and he tried just one. Oooops! Over went a full basket of eggs.

The exhausted chickens groaned. The rabbits shouted at Ralph. "Go play soccer on the other side of the trees so we can finish our work in peace," they said.

Ralph was glad to go. He
went off to play by himself on
the other side of the forest.

That night, he did not come home.

His mother wept and wrung her hands. "Where could he be?" she wondered. "And with Easter just two days away."

Morning came. Still Ralph had not come home. Liza slipped out to search for him.

She found him not far away— locked up in a cage.

A farmer had caught him while he was practicing his dribble in the cauliflower field.

"The coach always told us to look where we were going, not at our feet," Ralph joked sorrowfully.

"Don't worry," Liza told him. "I'll go and get help."

She ran back, past the busy rabbits, calling,
"Mama, mama, we must save Ralph. The farmer
has caught him and is going to make him into
Easter dinner!"

"Oh, I knew that bunny would get into
trouble someday," wept mama as she
followed Liza to Ralph's cage.

It had thick bars and a heavy padlock.

"We'll never get him out of there," moaned their mother when she saw Ralph inside.

"Of course we will," said Liza firmly. "I think I can get the lock open."

23

Liza worked for hours. But the lock refused to be picked. The bars wouldn't bend. The door couldn't be pried off.

24

"If I ever get free," whispered Ralph, "I promise I will never play soccer again."

"No, Ralph," said Liza, "you want to be a soccer player. And you will be, too. But you also have to help with the eggs."

"And not be such a nuisance," added mama.

Ralph knew they were right. He promised to do what they said.

Hours passed. Suddenly Liza cried, "I've got an idea that will do the trick! But we have to hurry."

Liza and mama ran all the way home. In no time, Liza was back carrying a small bundle under her arms. She squeezed it carefully through the bars of Ralph's cage. Then she whispered the plan.

The next morning there was a
great commotion around the cage.

Inside it, next to Ralph, was a basket of the most beautiful Easter eggs anyone had ever seen. Some were polka-dotted, some were dyed deep purple, and some were painted with rainbows.

The farmer's children gathered around. "He must be the Easter Bunny," they exclaimed with wonder. "How else could he have gotten those eggs? We must let him go or there won't be any Easter for us."

So the farmer opened the cage door.

Ralph ran home as fast as he could.

But he didn't forget Liza's words. He did try harder with his painting.

Ralph even became known for one special design, which he did far better than anyone else, and almost as well as kicking, passing, and scoring.

MORE
BUNNY
TROUBLE

On the day before Easter, Ralph was out kicking his soccer ball—just what he liked to do most.

Then his mother told him to watch his little sister Emily—just what he didn't like to do most.

He couldn't understand why his mother and father made such a fuss about Emily. She cried a lot and was always wet.

Ralph thought Emily must be the noisiest, messiest baby in the whole world.

Ralph's mother gave him some Easter eggs to decorate and a blanket to sit on.

"Be sure that your sister does not crawl into the tall grass," she told Ralph.

Ralph was trying to concentrate on his painting when Emily reached over to touch the eggs.

"Stop that!" Ralph said, and he poked her with his paw. Not too hard, but not too gently, either—just enough to make Emily cry.

Mama came running. "What's the matter with Emily?" she asked Ralph.

"I don't know," Ralph said, pretending to be busy painting an egg.

But Ralph's mother had a good idea of what had happened. "Ralph, I have told you over and over again— paws are not made for hitting."

Ralph bowed his head. "Yes, mama," he said.

But as soon as their mother was back inside, Ralph poked
his little sister again.

Emily cried and cried. But this time her mother did not come. Instead two butterflies flew by and fluttered around Emily's head.

She quickly forgot about the hurt and started after the pretty blue creatures.

Emily crawled off the
blanket and headed straight for
the tall green grass.

It was a whole new world
for Emily, filled with animals
and flowers she had never seen
before.

Everything was so pretty and
smelled so good. Emily looked
around, and then she went on
crawling. On and on....

Suddenly Ralph looked up and saw that
his sister was gone!

"Oh, no!" he cried. "I was supposed to be
watching her. Where did she go? How did
she get away so fast?"

"EMILY!" he called as loudly as he could.
"E-M-I-L-Y!" But there was no answer.

Ralph looked everywhere. He listened, trying to hear his sister's cry. Nothing.

"Oh dear! She must have gone into the tall grass! Anything could happen in there. A fox could get her, or an eagle, or a snake … I have to find her!"

But the grass was so tall Ralph could not see anything.

He ran to his mother and told her the whole story.

Ralph's mother did not lose any time. She called the neighbors together and asked them to help her find the baby.

All the rabbits were busy getting eggs ready for Easter. But this was more important. They stopped their work and ran out into the tall grass.

Each rabbit set off in a different direction.
The field was so large and there were so few
rabbits—how could they possibly search
every spot? Besides, in the thick grass, they
could easily pass right by the baby without
even seeing her.

"Emily! Emily!" they cried.

Still no answer.

Where was Emily? Could she hear them?

Someone did hear the rabbits calling. It was a fox!
He knew immediately what had happened.

He licked his chops. "With
a little bit of luck, I'll have
myself a delicious baby rabbit
for supper!" he said.

And with that, the fox
joined the search for little
Emily.

Emily's mother was getting frantic. "It's late," she cried. "We have to find Emily before the sun goes down."

"We need more help," said one of the neighbors. "The grass is so thick and tall and there are so few of us."

Then Ralph spoke up. "I know what we can do! Listen, everybody. I think I have the answer."

The rabbits stopped their search and gathered around Ralph.

"Here is my idea," Ralph said. "We will all hold paws together and walk in a long line across the field. That way we can cover every inch. We can't miss her."

All the rabbits thought this was a good idea. They joined paws and combed through the tall grass.

And that's how they found
little Emily, fast asleep, dreaming
of butterflies.

There were cheers as Ralph's mother took Emily into her arms again.

Everyone was overjoyed. Even Ralph shed a tear or two.

With the baby home safe at last, the rabbits could finish the Easter eggs in time.

It would be a happy Easter for all—except, of course, for the fox!

From then on, Ralph watched his
favorite sister very carefully.
    The two of them could often be
seen walking along, holding paws
together.

BAD, BAD
BUNNY
TROUBLE

Ralph was a bunny who loved soccer more than anything else in the whole wide world. He could play all day long, and he never wanted to stop.

"Ralph, come inside now," his mother called. "You have to get dressed for your sister's birthday party."

"Rats!" said Ralph.

It was the last thing he wanted to do.

"Look how dirty you are!" scolded his mother. "Quick, go upstairs and change. The guests will be here any minute."

Ralph saw that his mother was putting the candles on the birthday cake for Liza. She had also bought a coffee cake. Ralph wondered how it tasted.

Ralph was still angry at having
to leave his soccer game.

"This party would be more fun
if we could just play soccer instead
of sing stupid songs," he grumbled.
"We'll probably play stupid musical
chairs or pin the stupid tail on the
stupid donkey."

Ralph took his time getting ready.
He was the last one to join the party.

After everyone sang "Happy Birthday,"
Ralph's mother was ready to cut the cakes.
Ralph said, "I want a piece of coffee cake."

"No, you can't have coffee cake," said his mother.
"It's for the grown-ups. The birthday cake is
for the children."

"But I don't want birthday cake! I want coffee cake!"
Ralph cried and stomped his feet.

"No!" his mother said again.

Ralph was so angry, he could not control himself.
He did something awfully horrible.

"If I can't have it, then nobody can," he said
—and he spat on the cake!

That did it! Now Ralph was in
bad, bad trouble.

"Ralph, how could you!" his mother gasped.
"Up to the attic, this instant! I'll deal with you later!"

Ralph's cheeks were burning as he stomped up to
the attic. But he really didn't mind. The attic was the
workshop where the rabbits decorated Easter eggs.
It was a nice big room, just perfect for working on
his fancy footwork.

Suddenly Ralph heard
horrifying screams outside,
and from the distance
came a terrifying chant:

"Tasty bunnies, hop, hop, hop,
Are delicious in the pot.
Simmered, boiled, or as a stew!
Watch out! Here we come for you!"

Looking out the window, Ralph saw
three large savage foxes.
Now everyone was in bad, bad trouble.

Downstairs there was great trembling and crying. The rabbits locked the windows and bolted the doors.

Then they all went down into the cellar, which was the safest place.

In all the commotion, everyone forgot about Ralph.

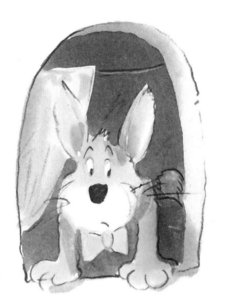

Ralph had to think fast.
He picked up a big basket of eggs
—and threw them out the window.

When the attacking foxes came running, they slipped and slid and skidded and toppled and crashed into each other in the gooey mess of broken eggs.

The foxes were not ready for this. Badly bruised and covered with slimy egg whites, they looked up and saw Ralph laughing in the attic window. They whispered among themselves and then disappeared into the bushes.

Soon the three foxes returned with a long, long ladder.
They started to climb up to the attic window.

But Ralph was prepared. He had lined up all the pails
of Easter egg dye, and one by one he dumped them
all over the foxes—first yellow, then blue,
then violet, and finally a big pail of bright red dye.

This was too much for the foxes. Grumbling,
they slunk back into the bushes.

"Victory!" cried Ralph, and he kicked
his soccer ball across the room.

But in the next moment,
Ralph heard and felt heavy thumps.
Everything in the room started shaking.
Now what was happening?

The foxes were back! And they were still trying to get in.

"Thump! Thump! Thump!
We're coming through
To have a bunny barbecue."

Ralph knew that now he needed some help. He thought of Brutus, the bull, inside the barn. But the barn was so far away.

There's just one chance, he thought.

Ralph placed his soccer ball
on the windowsill. This would be
the most important kick he had
ever made.

Ralph gave it all he had.

The ball arced and soared
and disappeared into the
open window of the barn.

"Ha, ha, ha! You missed us!"
laughed the foxes and they gave
the door another big thump.

Inside the barn, the animals were enjoying their afternoon snooze when the ball sailed through the window.

It bounced off the rooster's tail.

"Yikes-a-doodle-doo!" he cried as the ball headed for the hen.

"Squawk!" cried the startled hen, who accidentally laid an egg.

… which dropped on the pig and made
her little piglets squeal with laughter.
They giggled so hard that they knocked
over the milk can. Milk splashed
all over the billy goat.

Shaking and trying to kick himself dry,
the goat woke up the sheep and scared them so much …

… they fell against the ladder, which toppled over
and knocked down the bales of hay …

… which fell on …

84

… Brutus the bull!

Brutus had a terrible temper
and he didn't like to have his
nap interrupted.

He broke through the pen
and crashed out the barn door.
He was so mad that nothing
could have stopped him.

There was only one thing
Brutus hated more than being
disturbed when he was napping:
the color red.

And that was precisely what
he saw when he stormed out
into the yard—

Three fire-engine-red foxes!

Brutus galloped after them
and made them howl and
run for their lives.

Ralph knew that now the
foxes were gone for good.
"Atta boy, Brutus!"
he called from the window.
"We did it!"

The danger was over. The rabbits climbed out of the cellar. When they found out what Ralph had done, they gave him a big cheer. Then the happy rabbits celebrated not only Liza's birthday, but also their good fortune.

Liza told everybody, "Ralph must be the greatest soccer player in the world. Nobody else could have made a kick like that."

After everyone had a piece of birthday cake,
they all played a great game of soccer.

TEN LITTLE BUNNIES

Ten Little bunnies danced in a line.
Full of pep, one missed a step ...

Let's get this show on the road!

92

OOPS!

and then there were nine.

Nine little bunnies hopped through a gate.
Hippity hop, one couldn't stop…

Yippee!

BONK!

and then there were eight.

Eight little bunnies looked up to heaven.
Bzz! Bzz! What did they see? A busy bumble-bee …

STING!

and then there were seven.

Seven little bunnies carried some bricks
That wasn't easy, one felt so queasy …

and then there were six.

Six little bunnies went for a drive.
Vroom, vroom, a witch on a broom …

Check it out!

SWEEP!

and then there were five.

Five little bunnies knocked on the door.
Knock, knock, who's there? A big angry bear …

SLAM!

and then there were four.

Four little bunnies climbed up a tree.
Way, way up, a flying saucer and a cup …

O O S H!

and then there were three.

Three little bunnies went to the zoo.
Oh, what fun! There's the tiger—
Run! Run! Run!

That's no pussycat!

106

and then there were two.

Two little bunnies ate bun after bun.
Yummy! Yummy! One stuffed his tummy ...

BOOM!

and then there was one.

One little bunny, alone in a nook,
with one little stick and one magic trick …

Bonk!

Oops!

Help!

Swoosh!

Slam!

Whoosh!

Crash!

Boom!

Sting!

And look!

All ten little bunnies are back in the book!

CLICK!